The Problem with Cleo

written by Jenny Alexander
illustrated by Jim Kavanagh

Chapter One

Sam's Club

Cleo liked hanging around with the older ones. Some of the time, they didn't mind, because she could be funny and entertaining. But there were other times when they wanted to be on their own. The problem was, she wouldn't go away when they told her to.

One day, Sam had an idea she wanted to share with the others, but she didn't want Cleo to hear about it. She said Cleo was too young. She told the others to meet her in the secret room after school. Cleo didn't know about the secret room.

"What's this idea, then?" said Ben, as soon as they were all together. They had been dying to hear about it, because Sam had told them it was a really great idea.

"It's a new club," said Sam. "The Mischief Club. We can take turns thinking up good tricks to play on people. It'll be great!"

Ben didn't look convinced. "What sort of tricks?" he asked.

"Do you mean things like pulling people's chairs away when they're about to sit down?" said Jojo.

"Or tripping people up?" added Mouse.

Sam shook her head. That sort of trick wasn't any good, because someone could get hurt. They didn't have to hurt anyone in order to have fun. There were lots of things they could do for a laugh that wouldn't harm other people at all.

"Like what?" asked Ben.

"That's what we have to think of," Sam told him. "That's the challenge."

Ben, Mouse and Jojo weren't sure about the idea, but Donut was keen. "I think I've got an idea for a prank already!" Donut declared.

He was about to tell them his plan, when they heard a rustling sound in the bushes outside. They stopped talking, and listened. A twig snapped.

"There's someone outside," hissed Mouse. Sam crept up to the door and flung it open.

Cleo came tumbling in.

"What are you doing here, you little spy!" Sam snapped.

6

"And how did you know about the secret room?" demanded Donut.

Cleo stood up and brushed herself down. She had known about the so-called secret room for ages, she told them. "And now I know about your so-called secret club!"

"Well, you can't be in it. You're too young," Sam said, bossily. "So clear off!"

Cleo stuck her tongue out at them and then ran like the wind when they got up to chase her. They watched for a while to make sure she had really gone.

Then Donut told them his idea.

Chapter Two

Mrs Potter's Poodle

Donut had to fetch something from his house first, but the others went straight to Ben's. They got a packet of ginger nuts, and sat on the grass in front of his house, to wait.
There weren't many people about.

"Have I missed anything?"
Donut said breathlessly, when
he arrived. They shook their heads.
They asked him to show them
what he had got.

It was the frilliest little bonnet they had ever seen, with pink ribbons to tie under the chin.

"Cleo uses it when she's playing babies," he said.

Donut put the bonnet on Jojo's head, and everyone laughed. She put it on Mouse's head. They messed about with the bonnet until Donut finally took it back, helped himself to a ginger nut and sat down with the others. Ravi's shop was directly opposite, so they had a good view. Two girls from the secondary school went in to get some sweets. A bus went by.

At last, they saw Billy's
next door neighbour, Mr Timms,
walking up Story Street with his dog.
He tied the end of the lead to the hook outside
the shop, and went in. The friends looked at each other.

"It's a bit big," said Donut, doubtfully.

The dog saw them looking at him, and gave a small flick
of its tail. Ben said that he had read about a large dog that bit
someone's hand off. Sam said that was different – it must
have been someone the dog didn't know. "Dogs don't bite the
hand that pats them," she said.

"Shouldn't that be, 'the hand that feeds them?'" asked Jojo.

They were still discussing it when Mr Timms came out,
untied the dog and went back down the road, with his
newspaper under his arm.

"The bonnet wouldn't have fitted, anyway, said Donut,
as if that was the reason he hadn't done it.

Several ginger nuts later, they saw Mrs Potter come striding down the street with her poodle, Mitzi, trotting along beside her. They knew Mrs Potter, and they knew Mitzi. Neither of them was at all frightening. They didn't have to discuss it – they knew this was the one.

Mrs Potter tied Mitzi's lead to
the hook and went into the shop.
    As soon as she was inside,
Donut dashed across the road,
slipped the bonnet over Mitzi's
head and tied the strings
under her chin. Then he
came sprinting back.

Mrs Potter came out of the shop. She went to untie Mitzi, and jumped back in surprise. She stared and stared at the dog. She glanced up and down the road. She frowned. In Ben's garden, the friends were choking with laughter.

13

Just then, Mrs Potter's friend Edith arrived. They could hear snatches of the conversation. "Very pretty on her ... these hot days ... delicate dogs ... seems to like it ..." They chattered on for ages. Cleo came out of the shop, stopped to give Mitzi a pat and strolled across the road to where the others were hiding. She leaned against the fence.

Then Edith went into the shop, and Mrs Potter set off for home, not removing the bonnet from Mitzi's head. They watched her go. Suddenly, Sam stopped giggling. "What's Mitzi got on her tail?" she asked.

"Ha, ha! I put it on!" said Cleo. "I told you, I'm not too young!"

15

Chapter Three

A Very Unusual Duck

For Cleo to put her hair tie on Mitzi's tail right under Mrs Potter's nose while she was talking to her friend – that took some nerve, they all agreed. But if she expected them to let her join the new club, she was wrong. Although they had to admit she had a natural talent for mischief, they didn't like the sneaky way she had been spying on them.

"You'd better stop this right now," said Sam, "or there'll be trouble."

Cleo stamped her foot and stormed off, muttering that it wasn't fair.

At this point, Jojo felt they should perhaps let her join the Mischief Club. She already knew about the secret room, and she had shown she could be very daring. Mouse agreed. "It was her bonnet, too," he pointed out.

But Donut wasn't keen to have his little sister hanging around all the time. Ben thought they shouldn't encourage her to be naughtier than she was already. Sam was dead against letting Cleo join.

So they forgot about Cleo, and went back to the secret room to see if they could think of another prank to play. Jojo had the best idea. Everyone liked it because it was something they could all take part in.

"We'll tell everyone at school that a really unusual duck has been spotted on the lake in the park," she said. "We'll build it up really big, and say how beautiful it is and stuff. Then they'll all go and look for it after school ..."

"And it won't be there!" said Donut. "Brilliant!"

18

So after lunch the next day, the friends clustered together in the corner of the classroom, and talked to each other excitedly, as if something incredible had happened.

"I heard about it on the radio before school," Sam said.

"It was in the paper too," said Ben.

"Our mum says everyone at the City Farm wants to get a look at it." Jojo said.

Their classmates gathered round. "What?" they asked. "Get a look at what?"

Jojo turned round. "Haven't you heard?" she cried, pretending to be amazed. "Someone has spotted a really unusual duck on the pond in the park."

"It's the strangest-looking duck in the world, apparently," Sam said. "I can't wait to go down there and see it after school."

A buzz of excitement went around the classroom. When Mrs Duffy arrived, she wanted to know what was happening. They told her about the unusual duck.

"How interesting," she said. "I must borrow Mrs Turner's binoculars and go down and see it for myself. I'll go straight after school!"

The friends began to feel nervous. They had only meant to trick their classmates – they hadn't meant to trick their teacher, too. And things didn't improve when Mrs Duffy asked Mrs Turner at afternoon assembly if she could borrow her binoculars. As soon as Mrs Turner heard about the unusual duck, she said, "I'd like to see it too, Mrs Duffy. I think I'll come along with you."

By the time the bell went for the end of school, everyone had heard about the unusual duck. Half the children in the school, all the teachers and even some parents went down to the pond to look for it. They stood around talking in hushed voices for a while, until someone said the duck was probably hiding, because there were so many people about. Then they all lay down on the grass, or went to hide in the bushes.

Jojo and Mouse, Sam, Ben and Donut thought it was very funny, but they were too afraid to laugh. They didn't think all the people they had tricked would find it funny at all. But then someone cried, "There it is! Under the bridge! Look!"

They all looked at the bridge. In the shadows underneath it, something was bobbing about. It was bright yellow. As they watched, it floated out into the middle of the lake. Nobody said anything for a minute. Then everyone burst out laughing and talking excitedly.

27

The friends heard a movement behind them.

"It was my idea," said Cleo in a whisper. "You'll have to let me join your club now!"

Chapter Four

No, Cleo!

But the friends were really annoyed. "Will you stop sneaking around and spying on us?" they said. "Go away!"

Cleo was angry. She hung around and refused to leave them alone. They decided to get together again after tea, when Cleo wasn't allowed out.

They met in the secret room. It was seven o'clock and all the small children, the young couples and the people with dogs had all gone home.

"We need a new secret place," Sam said.

"Like where?" asked Ben.

Sam shrugged. They went for a walk around the park, to see if they could get any ideas.

When they had been right round several times, Sam said, "What about the big tree? We could climb up onto the lower branches. At least we'd be able to see Cleo from up there if she came snooping round." The others were doubtful about it. The tree looked hard to climb.

They all tried, but they couldn't quite manage it. Sam pulled the litter bin closer to the tree and climbed up onto it. She hoisted herself up onto the lower branch. Ben and Jojo went next, and then Donut and Mouse.

Then, just as they were all up the tree, Cleo popped out from behind it. She started to scramble up onto the litter bin.

"No, Cleo!" exclaimed
Donut, in alarm.

She stood on the bin and
stretched up, but she was too
short to reach the branch. She
stamped her foot on the bin
in frustration, making it
boom like a drum. Then she
slipped.

Cleo lay flat on her back beside the upturned bin, screaming
her head off. The others swung down out of the tree. They
tried to shut her up.

"Stop yelling," said Donut. "Tell us where it hurts."

"You'll get us all into trouble," Mouse added, nervously.

Cleo stopped yelling long enough to tell Donut it was her
neck that hurt. She told Mouse she didn't care if they all got
into big, big trouble. Then she started screaming again.

31

"We told you to stop following us," muttered Sam, angrily.

Ben looked worried. What if Cleo was really hurt? "Someone should go and get help," he said, breaking away from the group.

Sam grabbed his sleeve. "We can't! Cleo will say it was our fault," she said.

He shook himself free. "We'll have to take that chance."

32

Ben fetched Cleo's mum, Mrs Pringle. She brought her mobile phone with her. She took one look at Cleo, and dialled 999. She asked for an ambulance.

Sam said, "The hospital's only on the other side of the park – can't she walk?"

Mrs Pringle shook her head. Neck injuries could be very serious, she said, lowering her voice so that Cleo wouldn't hear. You should never move someone who had hurt their neck.

Mrs Pringle knelt on the ground beside Cleo and held her hand. "What on earth were you doing?" she asked.

Jojo butted in. "She was climbing on the litter bin ..." "We tried to stop her," added Sam.

Cleo had stopped yelling and started whimpering like a frightened animal. Her mother kept patting her hand and telling her everything was going to be all right.

At last the ambulance came. They heard it pull in at the entrance and, a few seconds later, two paramedics came running down the path towards them. They were carrying a rolled-up stretcher and a white plastic box with a red cross on the side.

Mrs Pringle explained what had happened. Then, one of the paramedics prepared the stretcher, while the other knelt down to talk to Cleo. "Don't you worry, little lady. You're going to be just fine," he said, soothingly. But Cleo just looked more frightened than ever.

35

He opened his box and took out a stiff plastic neck brace.
He told Cleo not to move – he and the other paramedic would
do all the work. He slipped the neck brace round her neck and
fastened it under her chin. Then the two men lifted her onto
the stretcher, and covered her with a blanket.

But they still weren't ready to go. They got two sandbags
and lay them on either side of Cleo's head. They put tape
across her forehead and round the sandbags, so that she
couldn't move her head at all. While they were working, they
explained what they were doing, and told her it was just
routine. There was nothing to be afraid of.

But Cleo still looked frightened and, as they carried her off
towards the ambulance, the friends looked frightened, too.

Chapter Five

Casualty

Inside the ambulance, there were seats on one side, where Donut and his mother sat, and a bed on the other. Cleo lay rigid on the bed, staring up at the ceiling. One of the paramedics travelled in the back with them. He fixed a clip to Cleo's thumb, and twiddled some knobs on a machine that looked like a radio. He talked to her about her favourite pop groups, trying to cheer her up. But she didn't look very cheerful.

When they got to the hospital, Nurse Lee was waiting for them. The paramedics put Cleo onto a trolley and wheeled her inside. Nurse Lee pulled back a curtain and showed them into an empty cubicle. "What have you been up to?" she asked Cleo. She had to lean right across, so that Cleo could see her.

"I was just climbing," Cleo said. "I wasn't even very high."

"Is it very painful?"

"It hurts when I move."

The nurse stroked Cleo's hand and told her she was a brave girl. Then she went to get the doctor.

It was ages before the doctor came. Donut and Mrs Pringle tried to keep Cleo amused, but she just cried quietly into her sandbags. In the end, Donut went to the waiting area to look for something to read to Cleo. They only had magazines and baby books. He took a board book, which looked about 500 years old. It was about a duck called Susan.

Cleo liked the story of Susan, and she made Donut read it twice. He had to hold it above her face, so she could see the pictures. When she got bored with the story, he went through it again, making up extra bits and changing the names.

"Soosie Poosie Poops popped to the shops. She got fresh fish fingers for her frog called Fred!"
By the time the doctor came, Cleo was actually laughing.

The doctor gently pulled the tape off Cleo's forehead and took the sandbags away. He undid the neck brace and slipped it out from under her neck. He asked Cleo to tell him exactly what had happened.

"I climbed up on top of a litter bin in the park," Cleo began.

"A litter bin?" he said.

"I was trying to climb a tree, and I couldn't quite reach the bottom branch."

Mrs Pringle looked astounded. "Honestly, Cleo! That's a really naughty thing to do. You should know better by now."

Cleo shrugged.

The doctor felt her neck with his fingers. He held her head and moved it slowly from side to side. He said she hadn't done any lasting harm, but she would have to wear a special collar for several weeks and do some exercises to help her neck get better. "It will be uncomfortable for a while, so I'll give you some medicine for the pain," he added.

Mrs Pringle phoned her husband and asked him to pick them up in the car. Now that she knew Cleo was going to be all right, she felt free to give her a proper telling-off.

"You sneaked out after tea, which you know you are not allowed to do, and then you did this stupid, ridiculous thing, trying to climb a tree that was much too high for you. What if you had managed it, and then couldn't get down again?"

Cleo looked sheepish. "I didn't think of that," she mumbled.

Donut hadn't thought of that, either. He was beginning to feel foolish, as well as guilty. But their mother was too busy cross-examining Cleo to notice him.

"What I want to know is this – why did you sneak out and go climbing trees? What on earth put that idea into your head?"

Chapter Six

Mr Pringle's Solution

While Donut was at the hospital with his sister, waiting for their dad to come and pick them up, his friends were in Sam's bedroom, waiting for him to get back.

From her window they could get a good view of the park, the hospital and Donut's house. They wanted to know as soon as Donut got home, so they could go straight over and find out what had happened.

Was Cleo all right?
Had she told on them?

The Pringles' car drew up outside their house. Donut and his dad were in the front. His mum and Cleo were in the back. As Cleo got out, the friends saw the neck collar gleaming white.

"At least she hasn't broken her neck, then," said Jojo. They all breathed a sigh of relief.

"All right," said Sam. "Let's go!"

But nobody moved. There was no way they could just see Donut on his own. If they went over, they were bound to see Mr and Mrs Pringle as well, and that felt too risky. Perhaps they should leave it until the morning, when things had had a chance to settle down.

The telephone rang while they were still debating what to do. It was Mrs Pringle. She wanted Sam to come straight round, she said. She wanted to have a word with her. Sam was trembling so much, she nearly dropped the telephone.

"I'd like to talk to Ben, Jojo and Mouse as well," said Mrs Pringle. "Do you know where they are?"

"They're here," Sam said, weakly.

Mrs Pringle asked her to bring them over with her.

45

The Pringles were in their living room, drinking tea. They seemed unusually serious and subdued. Mrs Pringle offered Sam and the others something to eat and drink, but they had suddenly lost their appetite. It didn't help that the cake looked like a frisbee with icing on. All Mrs Pringle's cakes had a tendency to be flat and hard. With a little more crunchiness, they could have been mistaken for biscuits.

Mrs Pringle told them to sit down. "First of all," she said, "I want to thank you for looking after Cleo while Ben came to find me."

They exchanged a glance, wondering what was coming next.

"Secondly, I'd like to talk to you about what Cleo was actually doing when she fell."

They braced themselves.

Mr Pringle took over. "Cleo has told us that she was trying to climb up the big tree ..."

"Which was a very silly thing to do, and we've obviously told her off about it," Mrs Pringle put in.

"It seems she was pretending the tree was a pirate ship, and she was trying to climb up to the crow's nest ..."

The friends looked gratefully at Cleo, and she shot them a secret grin. Mr Pringle didn't notice.

47

"The problem is," he went on, "that Cleo is always getting into scrapes because she seems to have no common sense at all ..."

"But I think I've got the solution," Mrs Pringle announced. "If she could spend more time with you older ones, I'm sure she would soon grow up a bit. You would be a good influence on her, and you could help her to stay out of mischief!"